D0364270

First published 1993 by Walker Books Ltd
87 Vauxhall Walk, London SE11 5HJ

© 1993 Nick Butterworth

Printed and bound in Singapore
by Tien Wah Press (Pte.) Ltd.

This book has been typeset in Century Old Style.

British Library Cataloguing in Publication Data
A catalogue record for this title is available
from the British Library.

ISBN 0-7445-2519-5

MAKING FACES

Written and illustrated by
Nick Butterworth

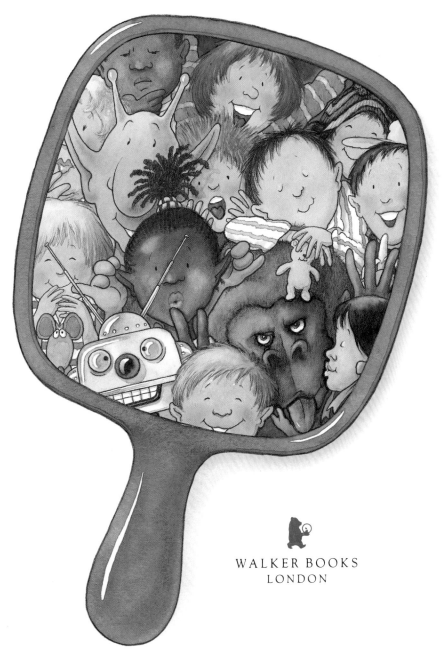

WALKER BOOKS
LONDON

Faces, Faces, Faces

Wherever you look you see faces.
People's faces. Animal faces.

Even cars seem to have faces.

The moon has a face. Clocks have faces.
And if you look carefully, you can see faces in
the clouds or in the shapes made by a fire.

Faces are fun to make.
You can draw them, or make model faces.

You can make them with sweets
or with fruit or leaves.

But the best way of making faces
is to use your own. So look in the mirror
at the back of this book and let's
get making faces!

Yucky Medicine

Just imagine, one morning
your mum says to you,
"You don't look very well, dear.
You look all pale and droopy."

🪞 Look in the mirror at your
pale and droopy face.

Then your mum says, "What you
need, dear, is a spoonful of
Dr Jollis's Strengthening Medicine."

Oh … yuck! You've had it before.
It's green. And lumpy.
It tastes disgusting.
Run and hide. Get on
the settee and look
like a cushion.

🪞 What does your
cushion face
look like?

It's no good. Your mum
has seen you.
Quick! Get under the
table and look like a cat.

 What does your
cat face look like?

Oh dear! There's no escape.
Here comes your mum.

And here comes a great big spoonful
of Dr Jollis's green, lumpy
Strengthening Medicine.
Look out!

Oh yuck! Yucky-yuck!
It tastes disgusting.

What does your
disgusting medicine
face look like?

Snow, Lovely Snow!

Just imagine a cold grey winter's day. You're not allowed to play outside. But look out of the window! It's snowing!

🔍 What does your face look like when you press it up against the window?

Surely you'll be allowed to play outside now? You ask very nicely. "Please, please, ple-e-e-ease!"

🔍 What does your asking nicely face look like?

The answer is yes! You put on your warm clothes and out you go into the garden.

Snow! Lovely snow!
First, you make a few snowballs.

Next door's cat is looking worried.

Well, how would you look if someone much bigger than you started making snowballs?

You've decided to make
a snow monster.
It's going to be huge
with a great big head.

It's very hard work.
It takes all day.
But at last it's finished.

Suddenly the lady who
lives next door looks
over the fence…

What face
does she make
when she sees
your snow monster?

The Moonman

Just imagine you're flying
to the moon in a spaceship.
It's a dangerous journey.
You have to be serious.

What does your serious
space pilot face look like?

You're nearly there now.
Be careful… Bump! At last you have landed.
You leave the spaceship to take a look round.

Look out! There's someone
coming. It's a moonman.
You're not scared, are you?

How do you look when
you're on the moon and
a moonman comes
and you're not scared?

The moonman looks sad.
He looks very sad indeed.

Can you look as sad
as the moonman?

The moonman is sad
because he has no friends.
He lives all alone
on the moon.

Well, that's no problem.
He can fly home with you.
Now he's got lots of
friends. He's happy now.

Can you look
as happy as the
moonman?

Slugs and Snails

Just imagine what it's like being very small, as small as a snail. You have to carry your house on your back and move very slowly.

🪞 Can you make a face like a snail?

Aha! Here come a couple of slugs. They look friendly.

🪞 Can you make a face like a slug?

The slugs haven't got fine houses on their backs like you. You must be very proud of your fine house.

🪞 What does your proud face look like?

Oh no! Here comes a bird.
It's one that eats snails.
You'd better hide inside
your shell.

⬭ What face
do you make
for hiding?

It's no good hiding. The bird has a long beak for poking
into shells. You'd better turn back into a person again,
as quickly as you can.

Phlooop! There! The bird is
very surprised. He's amazed.

⬭ Can you make an amazed
bird face?

The Fairground

Just imagine a fairground.
Sticks of rock. Candyfloss.
Toffee-apples. You've
had one of each.

What does
your sticky face
look like?

The roundabout rides are
great fun. How about a ride in a plane? You're flying
round and round very fast. Round … and round …
and round … and round.　　　　You're getting dizzy.

How do you look when you're dizzy?

Phew! Time for an ice cream.
You've chosen a very big one.
It has three flavours with a
chocolate flake. Mmmmm!

🪞 What face do you make
for delicious?

Now for a ride on the galloping horses.
Hold tight. We're off! Up and down,
round and round. Up and down,
round and round. Up and down…

Oh dear! Perhaps you
should have had a
smaller ice cream!

🪞 What do you look like when you're feeling sick?

Penguin's Joke

Just imagine these are your friends.
The penguin knows a joke. He thinks it's very funny.
He tells the joke to the rabbit and the rabbit thinks
it's funny too.

Can you laugh
like the rabbit?

Now the penguin tells the
joke to the bear.
The bear thinks the joke
is funny too.

🔍 Can you laugh
like the bear?

Everyone who hears the joke thinks that it's very funny.

🔍 Can you laugh like them? Like the mouse?
Like the giraffe? Like the robot?

One of your friends whispers the joke to you.
Do you think it's funny? What is the joke? Will you tell?

Tea with Auntie

Just imagine it's Sunday
afternoon and Auntie
is coming to tea.
Everyone has to look
smart, with faces washed
and hair combed.

What face do you
make when you're
having your hair combed?

Here comes Auntie now.
She's going to give you
a great big wet kiss!
Sssmwwch!
What a kiss!

What face do you
make when Auntie
kisses you?

At teatime Auntie
sits down.
Oh dear! Who left
a cream cake on
Auntie's chair?
Auntie doesn't
think it's funny.
Just look at
her face.

Can you
make a face
like Auntie's?

Everyone is trying not to laugh,
but it's very hard.

What do you
look like when
you're trying
not to laugh?

A Boring Day

Just imagine it's a boring sort of day. It's raining outside. You've got nothing to do. Your friend can't come to play. You're fed up.

How do you look when you're fed up?

You decide to do some colouring. You're colouring in a picture of a little cat wearing a big bow-tie. But you keep going over the edge. It's not your best colouring, so you make an angry face at the cat.

How do you look when you're angry?

Now you feel really horrible,
so you scribble on the picture.

Look at your horrible
face in the mirror.

DING DONG! There's someone at the door.
Who is it? Hooray! Your friend has come to play after all.
Even better
than that,
your friend
can stay
the night.
Yippee!

What face
do you make
for yippee?

On the Beach

Just imagine … the seaside.
The tide is out and the beach
is wide and flat. And you've
had an idea!

You dig the edge of your
spade into the sand
and start to draw lines.
You whistle as you work.

How do you look
when you whistle?

You're drawing a face. A great, big, long, thin face.

Can you make a face like this one?

What are you drawing now? It's enormous.
It's the biggest, fattest, funniest sand face ever!

 Can you make your face look fat and funny?

Oh dear. The tide is coming in again. The thin face is
getting wet around the eyes. It looks like it's crying.

 Can you pretend to cry?

What face do you make?

Never mind. Next time you come, there'll be
a brand new beach just waiting for you.

In the Jungle

Just imagine you're
exploring the jungle.
It's hot and dark and a
little bit scary.

What does your
jungle explorer's
face look like?

There are lots of noises
in the jungle.
Screeches and squawks.
Growls and roars.

Can you make a face
like a parrot?
Like a monkey?
Like a tiger?

You're feeling hungry. So you get out your packed lunch.
Look out! A huge gorilla is coming towards you.
He looks hungry too. You're afraid he wants to eat you.

What do you look like when you're afraid?

But the gorilla doesn't want to eat you.
He wants a bit of your banana. Yum!
Now the gorilla is your friend.

How do you look
  when you're in
the middle of the
jungle sharing a
banana with
a gorilla?

Father Christmas

Just imagine it's Christmas Eve.
You're feeling very excited.

What does your face
look like on Christmas Eve?

You hang up your stocking and
now it's time for bed. You want
to stay awake to see Father Christmas,
but you're very tired.

What do you look like
when you're very tired?

Listen!
What's that noise?
It's sleigh bells.
Father Christmas is coming.

You pretend
to be asleep,
but all the
time you keep
peeping from
under the covers.

What do you look like when you're peeping?

Father Christmas comes
into your room and stands
by your bed.
He chuckles to himself.
Do you think he knows
that you're awake?

Father Christmas
leaves a wonderful
present for you.

Look at your face in the mirror … it's the
biggest smile in the whole wide world!